KT-223-085

For Matthew and Andrew

Teggs is no ordinary dinosaur —
he's an **ASTROSAUR!** Captain of
the amazing spaceship DSS *Sauropod*,
he goes on dangerous missions and
fights evil — along with his faithful
crew, Gipsy, Arx and Iggy!

For more **ASTRO-FUN** visit the website:

www.astrosaurs.co.uk

www.**kidsatrandomhouse**.co.uk

Read all the adventures of
Teggs, Gipsy, Arx and Iggy!

BOOK ONE:
RIDDLE OF THE
RAPTORS

BOOK TWO:
THE HATCHING HORROR

BOOK THREE:
THE SEAS OF DOOM

BOOK FOUR:
THE MIND-SWAP MENACE

Coming soon

BOOK SIX:
THE SPACE GHOSTS

BOOK SEVEN:
DAY OF THE DINO-DROIDS

Find out more at www.astrosaurs.co.uk

Astrosaurs

THE SKIES OF FEAR

Steve Cole

Illustrated by Woody Fox

RED FOX

THE SKIES OF FEAR
A RED FOX BOOK: 978 0 099 48775 3

First published in Great Britain in 2006 by Red Fox,
an imprint of Random House Children's Books

7 9 10 8 6

Copyright © Steve Cole, 2006
Cover illustration © Steve Richards/Dynamo Design
Illustrations copyright © Woody Fox, 2006

The right of Steve Cole to be identified as the author of this work
has been asserted in accordance with the Copyright, Designs and
Patents Act, 1988.

All rights reserved. No part of this publication may be reproduced,
stored in a retrieval system, or transmitted in any form or by any
means, electronic, mechanical, photocopying, recording or otherwise,
without the prior permission of the publishers.

The Random House Group Limited supports The Forest Stewardship
Council (FSC), the leading international forest certification organisation.
All our titles that are printed on Greenpeace approved FSC certified paper
carry the FSC logo. Our paper procurement policy can be found at
www.rbooks.co.uk/environment

Set in Bembo Schoolbook

Red Fox Books are published by Random House Children's Books,
61–63 Uxbridge Road, London W5 5SA,
a division of The Random House Group Ltd
Addresses for companies within The Random House Group Limited can
be found at: www.randomhouse.co.uk/offices.htm

THE RANDOM HOUSE GROUP Limited Reg. no. 954009
www.**kids**at**randomhouse**.co.uk

A CIP catalogue record for this book is available from the British Library.

Printed in the UK by CPI Bookmarque, Croydon, CR0 4TD

WARNING!

THINK YOU KNOW ABOUT DINOSAURS?

THINK AGAIN!

The dinosaurs . . .

Big, stupid, lumbering reptiles. Right?

All they did was eat, sleep and roar a bit. Right?

Died out millions of years ago when a big meteor struck the Earth. Right?

Wrong!

The dinosaurs weren't stupid. They may have had small brains, but they used them well. They had big thoughts and big dreams.

By the time the meteor hit, the last dinosaurs had already left Earth for ever. Some breeds had discovered how to travel through space as early as the Triassic period, and were already enjoying a new life among the stars. No one has found evidence of dinosaur technology yet. But the first fossil bones were only unearthed in 1822, and new finds are being made all the time.

The proof is out there, buried in the ground.

And the dinosaurs live on, way out in space, even now. They've settled down in a place they call the Jurassic Quadrant and over the last sixty-five million years they've gone on evolving.

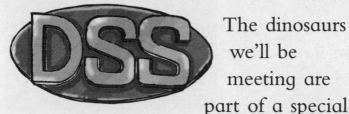

The dinosaurs we'll be meeting are part of a special group called the Dinosaur Space Service. Their job is to explore space, to go on exciting missions and to fight evil and protect the innocent!

These heroic herbivores are not just dinosaurs.

They are *astrosaurs!*

NOTE: The following story has been translated from secret Dinosaur Space Service records. Earthling dinosaur names are used throughout, although some changes have been made for easy reading. There's even a guide to help you pronounce the dinosaur names at the back of the book.

THE CREW OF THE DSS SAUROPOD

**CAPTAIN
TEGGS STEGOSAUR**

ARX ORANO,
FIRST OFFICER

GIPSY SAURINE,
COMMUNICATIONS
OFFICER

IGGY TOOTH,
CHIEF ENGINEER

Jurassic Quadrant

Ankylos

Steggos

Diplox

INDEPENDEN
DINOSAUR
ALLIANCE

vegetarian
sector

Squawk
Major

DSS
UNION OF
PLANETS

PTEROS'AURI

Tri System

Corytho

Lambeos

Iguanos

Aqua Minor

THE SKIES OF FEAR

Chapter One

THE LONG SQUAWK

It was midnight on board
the DSS *Sauropod*.
All was quiet as the
ship soared through
space.

A few astrosaurs
were working late.
Ankylosaurs tinkered
with the ship's mighty
engines. Stygimolochs mopped and
cleaned the corridors. The alarm
pterosaur made a cup of swamp tea to
help her stay awake.

And then a strange sound started up.
It was a weird, straining *ROAR* of a

sound. Like a T. rex trying to lay a two-ton egg. Like a thousand chickens singing from the bottom of a well. Like a billion beaks bashing at a battleship.

The sound blared from the *Sauropod*'s speakers all round the ship. The ankylosaurs dropped their tools in surprise. The shocked stygimolochs threw  their mops and buckets in the air. The alarm pterosaur screeched but no one could hear her over the dreadful din.

Captain Teggs Stegosaur jumped out of bed and galloped to the nearest lift, still in his pyjamas. He was a dashing, orange-brown stegosaurus who feared nothing – except perhaps an empty larder. For Teggs, the best things in life were eating and having adventures, ideally at the same time. But being woken at midnight by a sinister sound was enough to make even *him* lose his appetite.

As he reached the lift he saw that Gipsy Saurine had got there ahead of him. This bright stripy hadrosaur was in charge of the *Sauropod*'s communications. She took her hooves from her ears to salute him.

"Never mind that," Teggs told her. "If my hands could *reach* my ears, I'd cover them too! We've got to stop that terrible noise!"

5

"I'm sure the dimorphodon are working out what's going on right now," said Gipsy.

The dimorphodon, a type of pterosaur, were the *Sauropod*'s flight crew. There were fifty of the little flying reptiles on duty right now. With their nimble claws and delicate beaks they worked the ship's controls swiftly and surely.

Or rather, they *usually* did.

As Teggs and Gipsy burst out of the lift and onto the flight deck, they found the dimorphodon were standing as still as statues.

"What can have happened to them?" cried Gipsy.

"Quick, shut off the speakers," Teggs told her. "I think my ears are about to explode!"

Gipsy rushed to her post and pressed a button. A sudden silence fell over the flight deck. Then the lift doors swished open and a green triceratops burst in. It was Arx Orano, Teggs's first officer. He had dressed so quickly, he'd forgotten to take off his nightcap.

"Are we under attack?" he gasped.

"I don't know!" Teggs turned to Gipsy. "Any sign of enemy ships?"

"None, sir." She peered closely at her instruments. "The signal is coming from a long way away . . ."

"See if you can pinpoint the source of it," Teggs ordered. He was inspecting the dimorphodon. Their little eyes were goggly and glazed, and their beaks hung open.

"They're in some kind of trance," said Arx, sad to see his flapping friends in such a state. "That sound – perhaps it's some kind of weapon!"

"But *we* haven't been affected." Teggs frowned. "Have we?"

Just then, Iggy Tooth stomped out of the lift. Iggy was a stocky iguanodon, the *Sauropod*'s chief engineer. He was also very good in a fight – and it looked like he was ready for one now!

"I was having a brilliant dream about beating the raptors in a space-

car race," he grumbled. "Then that nasty noise made me fall out of bed! What *was* it?"

"We're trying to find out," said Teggs, crossing to Gipsy's side. "But first I'd better talk to the crew!"

"Good idea," Iggy agreed. "After a scare like that, we'll have enough extra dung on board to power the ship for a whole month!"

Gipsy flicked a switch and Teggs's voice boomed over the rattling speakers. "This is your captain! Don't panic. Everything is under control."

But suddenly the flight crew snapped back into life. They squealed and squawked and flapped all around, working the controls at top speed.

"What's got into them?" gasped Gipsy.

The floor lurched beneath their feet. "We're changing course!" said Arx.

"Stop it!" shouted Teggs. "We're on our way to meet Admiral Rosso at DSS Headquarters! You can't just steer us somewhere else!"

But the dimorphodon wouldn't listen.

Gipsy was astounded. "They've never disobeyed an order before!"

"*I'll* sort them out," said Iggy. He jumped up and grabbed the dimorphodon team leader – a plucky little reptile they nicknamed Sprite. "Stop that flapping and explain yourself!"

Sprite wriggled in Iggy's hands. He chittered and squeaked.

Gipsy spoke fluent pterosaur, and so she quickly translated. "He says that the sound we all heard was the Long Squawk."

"The *what*?" asked Teggs.

Again, Sprite clucked and squealed.
The rest of the dimorphodon waited in
mid-air, but Teggs could see they were
dying to get on.

"The Long Squawk is a special
signal, only sent in an extreme
emergency," Gipsy
explained. "It's an
urgent summons
from the High
Flapper!"

"The *who*?"
asked Teggs.

"The ruler of
Squawk Major, the pterosaurs' home
planet," said Arx. "Whatever's
happening, Captain, it must be pretty
serious. The Long Squawk hasn't been
heard for two hundred years. When
they hear the signal, all pterosaurs –
whatever their breed, wherever they are
– must return home at once."

"Return home at once!" cried the

alarm pterosaur over the speakers. "Full speed ahead! Return home at once!"

"I see what you mean!" said Teggs.

"I've traced the source of the sound, Captain," Gipsy reported. "It *is* coming from Squawk Major."

"The High Flapper must need help very badly," said Arx.

Sprite gave a sad little cheep.

Teggs nodded. "All right, Iggy, let Sprite go."

Sprite fluttered free with a grateful smile.

"And get your team to shovel all that fresh dung straight into the engines," Teggs continued. "We'll need it if we're going to stay at top speed all the way to Squawk Major."

Iggy saluted. "Right away, Captain!"

At once, the dimorphodon flapped back into action, working the *Sauropod*'s controls while Arx supervised.

"Won't Admiral Rosso be cross with

us?" wondered Gipsy.

"I'm sure he'll understand," said Teggs. "It sounds like this is a real emergency." He chomped on a beakful of ferns and smiled at the thought of a new adventure. "There's no time to lose!"

Chapter Two

IN A FLAP

As it turned out, Admiral Rosso was glad the *Sauropod* was already speeding to Squawk Major.

"You're captain of our fastest ship, Teggs," the old barosaurus remarked. "As soon as I heard the Long Squawk, I planned to send you there. You must help Lady Shazz, the High Flapper, in any way you can!"

Iggy was pleased too, once he'd had a nap. "Squawk Major is the planet next door to Morass Minor," he said. "They hold the Mammoth Space-Car Rally there every month."

Arx didn't know much about sport. "Do you mean 'mammoth' as in really big, or 'mammoth' as in large, woolly elephant-thing with tusks?"

"Both!" grinned Iggy. "Once we've sorted out this flap with the pterosaurs, maybe we could pop across and watch the races!"

"Maybe," said Teggs. He was worried. Lady Shazz had refused to say what was wrong until they could talk face to face.

"Approaching Squawk Major now, Captain," said Arx.

"A ptero-taxi just called," Gipsy added. "They're ready to pick us up,"

Teggs clambered out of his control pit. "Time to go," he said. "But first, Gipsy, put a call through to Alass."

"Connecting you now, sir," she told him.

"Yes, Captain?" asked Alass, as her face appeared on the main screen. She was the ankylosaurus in charge of security.

Teggs smiled. "Since the dimorphodon are coming to Squawk Major with Gipsy, Arx, Iggy and me, I'm leaving you in charge until we get back."

Alass gave him her smartest salute. "Understood, sir!"

"Right, then," Teggs told the rest of his crew. "Let's take that taxi!"

Spaceships were banned from the skies of Squawk Major. The planet's air was pure and fresh, and smelly engines would spoil it for the millions of pterosaurs flying happily through the sweet-smelling skies. So any visitors

wanting to land on the planet had to
leave their spaceship in orbit and take
a ptero-taxi – a special space-carriage
pulled by a team of pterosaurs.

Teggs, Arx, Gipsy and Iggy all
squeezed on board. The dimorphodon
and the alarm pterosaur flapped in
after them. Then the shuttle bay doors
swung open, and the two drivers – a
pair of rugged nyctosaurus in spacesuits
– flapped off into space, towing the
taxi behind them.

Squawk Major lay below them like a giant orange pudding, streaked with wisps of creamy white cloud. A little tear of joy trickled down the alarm pterosaur's beak at the sight of her home.

Soon they were soaring through the rosy skies.

"Where is everybody?" Teggs wondered. "This is a planet of flying reptiles. But I don't see anyone flying!"

"Maybe we're too high up," Gipsy suggested.

But as the minutes passed, the skies stayed empty. Sprite chirped worriedly.

The alarm pterosaur patted him on the head with her wing.

"We're only three miles above the ground," Arx reported. "It should be quite busy round here by now."

"Look on the bright side," said Iggy. "At least with an empty sky we can't possibly crash into anything!"

But suddenly, there were two noisy squawks from outside.

"What's happening?" cried Gipsy.

"The pilots!" Teggs pointed to the nyctosaurus through the window. "They've stopped flapping!"

At once, the ptero-taxi dropped like a stone.

"They'd better *start* flapping, and fast!" said Iggy.

The nyctosaurus screeched loudly.

"They can't!" cried Gipsy. "They – they say they've *forgotten* how to fly!"

"Forgotten?" Arx gulped. "How can that be? They were fine a minute ago!"

The carriage was falling faster and faster.

"If they don't remember soon, we'll all be squashed flat!" cried Iggy. "And so will anyone beneath us!"

"We've got one chance," said Teggs. He whacked his spiny tail against the window and smashed out the glass. "Dimorphodon – take over!"

At once, Sprite led the valiant flight crew outside. Flying against the wind, they managed to take control of the

taxi from the
helpless
nyctosaurus. The
dimorphodon
were far smaller,
of course, but
there were fifty of
them. They started
flapping for their lives
– and the lives of their captain
and crew!

"We're slowing down!" gasped Arx.
"But not fast enough!"

Gipsy shut her eyes as the ground
came rushing up to meet them.

Then the alarm pterosaur, who was
not the bravest of flying reptiles,
hopped out through the window.
Flapping furiously, she lent her wings
to the struggle.

With a rush of relief, Teggs felt the
carriage coming back under control.
"They're doing it!"

"Thank goodness," beamed Gipsy, as the flock of pterosaurs towed them onwards. "We're going to be all right!"

Iggy wiped his brow. "And I'm going to keep my mouth shut for the rest of the trip!"

But Arx was still lost in thought. "How can a pterosaur forget how to fly? That's like Captain Teggs forgetting how to eat!"

"Pardon?" said Teggs through a mouthful of ferns.

The nyctosaurus could no longer fly, but at least they could give directions. Puffing and panting, the dimorphodon and the alarm pterosaur steered the carriage to the majestic home of the High Flapper – the Palace of Perches.

It towered over the castles and courtyards of the pterosaur city. It was beautifully built from bright blue rock, and was as big as a cathedral. Hundreds of stone flagpoles jutted from the walls, which were covered in carvings of beasts and birds.

"There's no door," said Teggs. "How do we get in?"

"Through the roof!" said Arx.

They circled overhead and swooped down through a large hole in the great glass ceiling. Inside, was a single, enormous room, filled with fruit trees and flowers. And there, right in the middle, sat the enormous Lady Shazz, the High Flapper.

Perched on a giant purple cushion, she was a regal sight: a crown upon her head, her long beak raised skyward, her leathery wings stretched out wider than a jet plane.

The ptero-taxi touched down beside

her. At once, servants flapped over with cool drinks and insects for the exhausted pilots.

Teggs led the others from the carriage, and bowed. "Greetings, your Highness."

"Greetings, astrosaurs," trilled Shazz. (Being the High Flapper, she spoke fluent dinosaur.) "Thank you for coming all this way."

"We would have got here sooner," said Teggs. "But halfway here, your pilots forgot how to fly!"

"Oh no!" Shazz slumped back onto her cushion. "Not them too! My last pair of plucky pilots!"

Arx frowned. "You mean this has happened before?"

"It's been happening for weeks!" she sighed. "Every day, millions more of us forget how to fly!" She gave a miserable squawk and buried her beak in her massive wings. "However hard they try, they simply can't remember how to do it!"

Chapter Three

THE COMING OF GRANDUM

"So that's why the skies are empty," Iggy realized.

Gipsy couldn't believe it. "But they're pterosaurs! Surely they can learn how to fly again?"

"They've tried and tried but they just can't get the hang of it." Shazz shed a silvery tear. "This morning, I thought I would fly over and teach some of them myself. But I fell flat on my face! Even *I* have forgotten how to fly! A High Flapper without her flap!" She wiped her long beak on an even longer wing. "And as if all this wasn't bad enough, the Trials are almost due to start!"

"Trials?" asked Teggs.

"The High Flapper Trials!" Shazz wailed. "I have ruled Squawk Major for almost ten years. According to pterosaur law, it is time for a new High Flapper to be chosen. A special contest will be held on Beak Mountain in one week's time. It is open to all flying reptiles. They will compete for the crown in trials of skill, strength and speed . . . But so far, not one person has entered!"

Arx nodded. "Because none of them can fly!"

"That is why I sent the Long Squawk alarm call into space," Shazz explained. "I have called back pterosaurs from all over the Jurassic Quadrant to take part!"

The dimorphodon and the alarm pterosaur squawked in surprise.

"And here comes one now!" cried Gipsy. "Look! Up there!"

A dark cloud had gathered over the palace, and an even darker shape was swooping out of it. It was an enormous flying reptile, the size of an elephant. Its wings were like huge hairy sheets, and bigger than a jumbo jet's. Its body was broad and fat. Its head was long and leathery with a big, bent beak.

Whoosh! It dropped right in through the skylight!

"What a cheek!" gasped Shazz.

"What a *pong!*" Teggs complained. The

31

new arrival stank of dung and grease and engine oil. "I could smell him a mile away!"

The dimorphodon scattered as the giant reptile landed on top of their carriage – and squashed it flat!

Shazz screeched in outrage. "How dare you enter my palace unannounced!"

The newcomer smiled slyly. "Just checking out my new home," he said. "Hmm. Needs some decorating."

"New home?" Teggs stamped over to face him. "But this is the Palace of Perches! The High Flapper lives here!"

"Exactly. And once I've won the Trials, I will *be* the High Flapper, won't

I?" He threw back his beak and laughed. "My name's Grandum. I was enjoying the racing on Morass Minor when I heard the Long Squawk. Thanks for the tip-off, darling – I came at once!"

Arx bustled forwards crossly. "You can't call the High Flapper 'darling'!"

"Can't I?" Grandum frowned. "How about 'Bootface'?"

"Bootface!" Shazz squawked in horror.

"You're the rudest reptile I ever met!" stormed Gipsy.

"Don't get your scales in a skid, sweetheart!" said Grandum. "I bite the tails off ugly dinosaurs like you and eat them for breakfast!"

"You are nasty and rough!" Shazz

declared. "Not fit to be High Flapper!"

"We'll see about that." His saucer-eyes were agleam. "I'll take on anyone in the Trials. Anyone!"

Teggs raised his tail in warning. "I think you should leave, Grandum. Now."

"Fine! You lot are boring me stiff, anyway!" He unfurled his enormous hairy wings. "But I'll tell you this. Once I'm in charge, there will be a lot of changes round here. None of this nicey-nicey rubbish. Everyone will do exactly what I say . . . or else!"

With that, and a very rude noise, he took off – leaving only a nasty whiff in his wake.

"You rotten, stinky devil!" cried

Shazz. She jumped off her cushion and beat her mighty wings as hard and as fast as she could – but it was no good. She couldn't fly a millimetre.

Exhausted, she flopped to the floor while her servants fetched water and fish and fresh crunchy bugs to revive her. "Oh dear!" she sighed. "What am I to do?"

"I think you should cancel the Trials," said Teggs. "At least until things are back to normal."

"I can only do that if the people all agree," said Shazz. "I had better call a Meeting of the Flock for tomorrow, so I can explain it to them."

Arx watched with interest as she crossed to a strange device that stood by a window. It was a cross between a long glass beak and a telescope, with a big red switch on the side. "That looks like a high-speed sound-o-scope," he said. "Is that how you made the Long Squawk?"

"Yes. It sends my voice all over the planet, even into outer space," said Shazz. She cleared her throat, turned on the sound-o-scope, and began to screech and cluck and whistle to her people.

"She's doing the right thing," said Gipsy. "I'm sure no one will mind if the contest is cancelled."

"I can think of someone who will mind a lot," said Arx. "Grandum!"

Teggs said nothing. He was looking worriedly up at the sky. It was empty except for more storm clouds, gathering overhead.

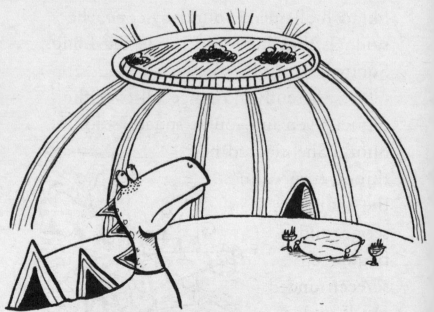

Chapter Four

THE MEETING OF THE FLOCK

The astrosaurs spent the night in the Palace of Perches, as Shazz's guests of honour. They were each given a solid gold perch. The dimorphodon and the alarm pterosaur were delighted, although the others were a bit worried about rolling off in their sleep.

As it turned out, Teggs couldn't sleep anyway.

The mystery of the forgetful flappers was bothering him too much.

As the dawn broke through the window overhead, he could see the sky was even cloudier this morning.

"Funny," Teggs thought. "That cloud looks just like one I saw last night . . . "

Yawning, he decided to find something to eat. He trotted up a steep stone staircase, and soon found a set of doors painted bright red.

"I wonder if this is the larder?" thought Teggs.

It wasn't.

He emerged onto a big balcony. It must have been a mile above the ground. And gathered in the square before him were thousands of grounded pterosaurs – all breeds and shapes and sizes, squashed up in silence together as far as the eye could see. Short little sordes, quirky quetzalcoatlus, wriggling rhamphorhynchus . . .

As soon as they saw Teggs, they squawked and threw little silvery missiles at him. The whole palace shook with the sound of their screeching. Moments later he was half-buried beneath about a billion slimy fish!

"Leave off!" spluttered Teggs. "I'm a vegetarian!"

Then Shazz came up behind him. "What are *you* doing here?" she asked in surprise.

"Look out!" cried Teggs, as more fish rained down. "We're under attack!"

"We most certainly aren't!" she said, snaffling some mackerel with her long beak. "This is how my people greet their High Flapper at a Meeting of the Flock — with a squawk of salute and the gift of fish! You've spoiled my big entrance!"

"Sorry," he murmured sheepishly, skidding on skipjacks to the back of the balcony.

Shazz climbed up the fish pile to greet her people. "Welcome, my flock," she called. "I know it was hard for many of you to get here without working wings."

There were bitter coos and clucks of agreement from the crowd.

"Is there *anyone* here who can fly?" asked Shazz.

Not a single wing was raised.

She sighed. "In that case, I say we postpone the High Flapper Trials until everyone is better and flying high again."

"And what if you *never* get better?" boomed a voice from above.

A gasp went up from the crowd. Teggs narrowed his eyes.

It was Grandum.

"She's tricking you!" cried the hairy, smelly pterosaur. "Shazz doesn't *want* you to fly! She wants to be High Flapper for ever!"

"That's not true!" bellowed Teggs.

"What do *you* know about it, *dinosaur?*" jeered Grandum. He turned back to the crowds. "*I* can fly! Nothing can stop me! Let the Trials go ahead – I'll compete against anyone! And if I'm made High Flapper, I'll show all of you how to fly again . . . which is more than Shazz can do!"

Eager whispers rustled through the crowd.

"We want to fly!" someone called.

"It's easy when you know how!" Grandum told them. "And I do!"

"This pterosaur is nasty and mean!" Shazz cried. "He will make you his slaves!"

"Rubbish," said Grandum. "She's lying. She knows I'm best and she can't stand it!"

"Let the Trials go ahead!" someone shouted. And soon, a ragged chant started up. It grew louder and louder: "*We want the trials! We want the trials!*"

Grandum chuckled. "Well, Bootface?"

Teggs stared at Shazz helplessly.

She lowered her head in defeat. "If the people wish it . . . the Trials must take place!"

The crowds clapped and whooped once more. But now it was Grandum they were cheering. He had sneakily won over the frightened crowd. Teggs scowled as he watched the enormous reptile do a victory dance in mid-air.

He could feel it in his bones . . . in the tiniest dimples of his tail spikes . . . There was more to Grandum than met the eye.

As the cheering went on, Teggs gently led Shazz back into the palace where the other astrosaurs were waiting.

"We heard everything," said Gipsy. Her head-crest had flushed purple with gloom.

"*Someone's* got to stand up to Grandum," Iggy declared. "But who?"

"What about Sprite?" Arx suggested.

"He's a gutsy little guy," Teggs agreed. "I'd be sad to lose him from the *Sauropod* if he won, but . . . "

He tailed off. Sprite squawked as he led the dimorphodon down the steps. They all looked miserable, with puffy eyes and runny beaks.

"Oh no!" cried Shazz. "Even *they*
have forgotten how to fly!"

Iggy stared at the dimorphodon.
"Lads, what happened? You were fine
yesterday!"

The whole flock shrugged helplessly.

"What about the alarm pterosaur?"
asked Teggs.

At the sound of her name she
appeared heroically at the top of the
steps. She launched herself into the air
and flew gracefully for a few moments
. . . then fell like a brick. Teggs winced
as she landed rather painfully on one
of Arx's horns.

"You poor thing," said Gipsy kindly, lifting her free. "Go and have a lie down."

"Lie down," she agreed. "*Squaaawk!*" And she waddled stiffly away.

"It's hopeless," sighed Iggy. "If only *you* could fly, Captain. You'd soon sort out that grotty Grandum."

"Me?" Teggs stared at him. "Iggy, you're a genius!"

Iggy blinked. "I am?"

Teggs nodded, grinning. "We've got just one tiny chance of stopping whatever Grandum's up to. But  we'll have to work fast and we'll have to work hard. Are you with me?"

Gipsy, Arx and Iggy proudly saluted. "As always!"

And so Teggs explained what they needed to do . . .

Chapter Five

THE TRIALS BEGIN

One week later, pterosaurs from all over Squawk Major gathered on Beak Mountain to watch the High Flapper Trials. Normally they would simply fly to the summit and watch from one of the many million perches. Now they had to walk, or cycle, or hang-glide from the nearest hills. It took them quite a long time.

But most pterosaurs decided to stay at home. What was the point of going to watch?

Grandum was the only one taking part!

Chief Judge Floss was in charge of the Trials. He was an elderly quetzalcoatlus with grey, leathery skin. He had helped to choose *twelve* High Flappers in his long life, and Shazz had been the greatest of all. He sighed. Grandum was not his idea of a good replacement.

The huge, smelly pterosaur was grinning like a gargoyle beside the winner's podium. "Why are we waiting?"

"The Trials will begin as soon as Lady Shazz arrives," said Floss.

"She's probably too busy blubbing in her palace 'cause she knows I'm best," laughed Grandum. "Tell you what, grandpa – why don't you just make me High Flapper now? No one else is coming!"

"*Someone* is!" gasped a voice in the crowd. "Look!"

"Someone else can fly!" cried another. "They are flying this way! And they're bringing . . . the High Flapper!"

Floss looked up in wonder. Grandum looked up in fury.

A funny-looking flying reptile was sweeping towards the summit of Beak Mountain. It was about the size of a stegosaurus, and covered in red

feathers. Its wingspan was the length of a double-decker bus. Shazz dangled proudly in its enormous claws.

"This is my champion!" Shazz declared as the newcomer gently set her down beside the judges. "He has come to enter the Trials!"

"My name is Flappo the Fearless!" boomed the big red pterosaur. The flocking crowds cheered and clapped.

Floss smiled at Grandum. "Looks like you have competition after all!"

"I'm not scared," sneered Grandum. "I'll squish him! Squash him! Marmalize and mash him!"

"This isn't a wrestling match!" said Floss sternly. "These are trials of skill."

"Then I'll squish him skilfully!" Grandum cried.

"Let's just get on with it," said Flappo. "Before you bore everyone to death!"

The crowd laughed and clapped their

wings. Grandum's eyes narrowed. He was sure he'd seen this Flappo character somewhere before . . .

And he had.

What Grandum didn't know – what *nobody* knew – was that Flappo the Fearless didn't exist.

It was Teggs in disguise!

Teggs didn't like tricking people, and he hated cheats. But he wasn't doing this to help himself. He had to save the people of Squawk Major from a wicked would-be ruler.

All the astrosaurs had been very busy over the last week. Gipsy had designed a special flying costume for Teggs, and the dimorphodon had stitched it together. The wings were mechanical and remote-controlled, built by Iggy and hidden by feathers. Thanks to a special camera in the beak, Iggy could

see everything Teggs could — which allowed the clever iguanodon to steer his captain through the skies with ease. There was also a two-way radio so they could keep in touch — along with one or two other useful gadgets . . .

Meanwhile, Arx had been running special tests on lots of pterosaurs who had forgotten how to fly. Teggs had hoped that if a cure could be found, he might not need to take part in the Trials at all. But it wasn't so simple.

"I can't see a thing wrong with any of these people," Arx had sighed, the night before the Trials. "They *should* be able to fly. The problem isn't in their wings — it's in their heads!"

Now Teggs looked sadly round at the crowd. He hoped Arx could solve that problem soon. And he hoped no one found out he was really an astrosaur in a pterosaur suit. That would get him disqualified at once!

Floss took his place between his junior judges, Moss and Joss. "Let the Trials commence!" he cried.

The crowds cheered and clapped, happy to be distracted from their woes for a while.

"The first Trial is the Trial of Squawking," Floss went on. "From one mile high you must give your best squawk. You will be marked on loudness, pitch and overall quality. Good luck!"

Grandum went first. With a rude noise and a smelly pong he burst into flight. Soon he was only a speck in the cloudy sky.

"Hooooooooo— arrrrrrrrrrrrrrrrrrhhhhhhhhhhhh- wuurrrrrrrrrk!" came an echoing squawk from on high. It was loud and clear and pleasing to the ear. The crowd clapped with enthusiasm.

"Beat that, fatso!" said Grandum rudely as he flapped back down to earth.

Teggs simply raised his front legs and hoped Iggy was ready at the remote control. His wings flapped a couple of times, then he felt himself lifting up into the sky. His flight was a bit wobbly, since he and Iggy hadn't had much time to practise. But no one seemed to notice as he hurtled up towards the clouds.

"Can you hear me, Captain?" said

Gipsy over the two-way radio.

Teggs looked down at the dizzying view of the mountain far below, and quickly wished he hadn't. "Loud and clear."

"Switch on your loudspeaker," she said.

Teggs flicked a switch hidden in his false beak, and heard Gipsy take a deep breath. Long ago, in the wild, hadrosaurs used their hollow head-crests to boost their voices when calling to their herds. It was a trick they could still use today.

*"Arrooooooooooo—
aaaaaaaaaaaahhhhhhhhh—grrrrrrrruk-
ooooooooh!"*

Gipsy's amplified hoot was incredible.
It nearly took Teggs's ears off. The
sound echoed for miles and miles. It
even started an avalanche on another
mountain nearby.

Chuckling to himself, Teggs was
steered back down to the summit,
where the crowds were applauding
wildly. Grandum was fuming with rage.

Floss conferred with Moss and Joss.
"And the results are . . . Grandum:
seven points. Flappo: *nine* points!"

Again, the audience burst into excited
applause. Grandum pretended to clap,
like a good loser – though he was
clearly furious. "You won't be leading
for long," he hissed. "It's the Trial of
Acrobatics next, and I am *hot*!"

"Is that why you're so smelly?" Teggs
asked innocently. But as the Trial

began, his tummy was doing acrobatics of its own. Could Iggy match Grandum's skill by remote control?

Grandum took off with another rude noise and instantly looped the loop. The crowds clapped and gasped as he spun and spiralled over their heads like a big, hairy boomerang. He flew straight up in the air like a rocket, then did seventeen somersaults on his way back down to the summit. The crowd happily squawked their approval.

"You see, Flappo? These fools love me," sneered Grandum, panting for breath. "I'll soon have them all in my power – and you too!"

"We'll see about that," said Teggs.

First, he took off *backwards*! Then he did a flapping flip in mid air and performed a double loop-the-loop. The crowd went crazy as he zigzagged through the sky, flying higher and higher.

Iggy chortled over the earpiece. "These mechanical wings handle like a dream!"

"More like a nightmare to me," groaned Teggs as his flying suit sent him through *twenty* perfect somersaults. "I feel air-sick!"

At last he started to spiral stylishly back down to the mountain-top, before landing as light as a feather.

The crowd's applause almost started another avalanche.

"Grandum scores eight points," Floss declared. "But Flappo scores *nine* points!"

"Bravo, my champion," called Shazz over the happy squawking of the great flock. "Now, let's break for lunch!"

But Grandum poked his beak in Teggs's ear. "Think you're clever, don't you?" he hissed. "Well, no one makes a fool out of me, Flappo! You're going to find the rest of the Trials a lot tougher. Just you wait!"

Chapter Six

RIDDLES, RIDDLES, RIDDLES

Teggs was dismayed to find that lunch was a fish and woodlouse salad. As he picked out the fish and woodlice and tried to suck lettuce up his false beak, he noticed Grandum wasn't eating. Instead the big bully was talking to a pair of shifty-looking woolly mammoths.

"What are mammoths doing here?" he wondered.

"Grandum came here from Morass Minor, home of the mammoth Space-Car Races," Iggy reminded him over the radio. "He must have brought some friends with him to cheer him on."

"I suppose so," said Teggs. When Grandum saw his enemy watching, he and the mammoths moved off into a nearby cave.

Once the food was finished, Teggs flapped over to meet Iggy and Gipsy in Shazz's royal carriage further down the mountain. This was their only chance to make any repairs to his flying suit. The two astrosaurs grinned and cheered as their captain came inside.

"How does it feel to be a top-class pterosaur?" asked Gipsy.

"Give me four legs on the ground anyday!" Teggs felt hot, sick and sweaty in his suit of feathers. "No offence, Sprite!"

The dimorphodon cheeped and saluted. He was sitting in the corner building his own set of robotic wings.

"He's making new wings for *all* the dimorphodon," Iggy explained. "They'll do anything to fly again!"

"They may be small, but they're plucky!" said Teggs fondly. Then he sighed. "You know, beating Grandum is only half the battle. We have to beat whatever is ailing the pterosaurs too. Any word from Arx?"

"Not yet," said Iggy, oiling Teggs's wings. "He's still hard at work back at the palace."

"I'm sure we'll hear something soon,"
said Gipsy, sewing up a small tear in
the suit. "Now, it's the Trial of Riddles
next. Good luck!"

"I'll need it," Teggs groaned. "I'm
rubbish at riddles! Grandum was right,
I *will* find the next Trials harder!"

"He was just trying to scare you,"
said Iggy.

But Teggs couldn't help thinking there
was more to it than that.

Teggs was soon back at the summit.
He landed next to Shazz.

"Hello, *Flappo*," she said with a wink.

"You haven't seen Chief Judge Floss anywhere, have you? Moss and Joss can't find him."

"There he is," said Teggs, pointing. "With Grandum and that mammoth!"

Shazz turned up her royal beak. "Why would he want to talk to *them*? And how come he's suddenly got so much fatter?"

"He must have really enjoyed his lunch," said Teggs enviously.

"He doesn't *look* like he enjoyed it," said Shazz. "His face has gone all wrinkly. It almost looks as if he's wearing a mask!"

"Right," said Floss gruffly, plonking his portly body down beside Joss and Moss. "Contestants, take your places on the puzzle perches."

The puzzle perches were each carved in the shape of a question mark.

Grandum perched on one, Teggs on the other.

"Right, then. Riddles. Here we go." Floss picked up the question card. "Flappo — what can't you see but is always ahead of you?"

Teggs mind went blank. "Er . . ."

Then Gipsy hissed over the radio: "The future!"

Teggs grinned. Of course! "The *future* is always ahead of you, though you can't see it!"

The crowd clapped politely.

"How dreary!" yawned Grandum. "The proper answer is – *an invisible narg*. You can't see an invisible narg but it's always ahead of you."

"It is not!" Teggs protested.

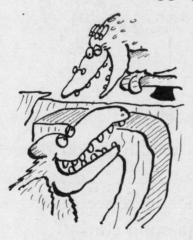

"Prove it!" chuckled Grandum. Even Chief Judge Floss roared with laughter. "An invisible narg is the correct answer!"

Joss turned to Floss. "What *is* an invisible narg, anyway?"

"If you don't know *that*, you shouldn't be sitting here at all," said Floss sniffily. "One point to Grandum. Nothing at all for Flappo."

"But that's not fair!" cried Joss.

"It's an outrage!" added Moss.

"Who is the Chief Judge around

here?" said Floss, with a menacing glint in his eyes.

Teggs's feathers bristled. He knew that his answer was right. What was Floss playing at?

"Next riddle," bellowed Floss. "Flappo, if you were pushed downstairs, what would you fall against?"

Teggs shut his eyes and tried to think. Grandum started humming smugly like he knew the answer.

"I know!" cried Teggs. "If you were pushed downstairs, you'd fall against *your will*!"

Again, the audience clapped and cheered.

But Grandum shook his head. "I think you'll find the *real* answer is that you'd fall against your big feathery bottom!"

A great gasp went up from the crowd.

"Correct!" cried Floss.

An even greater gasp went up.

Shazz gave him a hard stare. "Are you feeling OK?"

"Never better," Floss chuckled. "Two points to Grandum. Nothing to Flappo!"

"Er, surely Flappo deserves at least *half* a point?" Joss protested.

"His answer was very clever," said Moss.

"Softies," Floss snarled. "He can have a *quarter* of a point! Nothing more!"

Teggs's beak flapped open in disbelief. A wave of startled clucks and squawks went through the crowd. Nothing like this had ever been seen at a Trial before.

But Grandum was cool and calm, relaxing on his perch like a pterosaur whose troubles were over . . .

Back at the palace, Arx was taking a walk in the gardens to clear his head. He had been thinking so hard his horns were aching. He had tested the pterosaurs till he was blue in the face. But he simply couldn't figure it out. How could flying reptiles forget how to fly in a matter of moments? Why so many all at once – even members of the *Sauropod* crew? And how come none of them could learn how to fly again, except Grandum?

He glanced up at the sky. That was another thing – how come the clouds never seemed to move here on Squawk Major?

Despairing, he paused beside a royal pool. Fish were darting through the clear blue water, their scales glinting and glittering. Arx stared at the whirling patterns they made. The way they moved was almost hypnotic . . .

He blinked.

Hypnotic?

"That's it!" he yelled, and the fish scattered. "Someone has *hypnotized* the people into forgetting how to fly! One by one they've all fallen under a spell. That's why lessons made no difference!" He clapped his heavy feet together, then frowned. "But how could anyone hypnotize an entire planet?"

And an awful thought struck him.

Shazz used a high-speed sound-o-scope to send messages around the planet or out into space. What if someone was using a similar device to send a hypnotic signal all  over Squawk Major? A signal that was too high to be heard but which went to work directly on the brain – convincing the people of Squawk Major that they could not fly, even though they really could.

A *hypno-beam*!

Almost hoping he was wrong, Arx rushed back inside the palace to the sound-o-scope. It was the work of minutes to reverse the settings so it could *receive* signals. And by boosting the sound frequencies he could hear any secret messages.

Soon he heard a quiet, sinister voice broadcasting over and over: ". . . forget how to fly . . . You will forget how to fly . . . You will forget . . ."

Arx nodded grimly. He didn't know where the hypno-beam was coming from. He didn't know how he could stop it. But one thing he *did* know – the voice sounded a lot like Grandum's.

Chapter Seven

HEAD IN THE CLOUDS

Back at the Trials, Teggs was finding it hard going. Whatever he did, however good he was, however much the crowd cheered him on – Chief Judge Floss would always rule against him!

"He wasn't like this before lunch," Teggs grumbled to himself. "It's like he's become a completely different person!"

In the Trial of Swiftness, Teggs beat Grandum in the two thousand metre flying race by two seconds. But Grandum complained the wind had been blowing against him – so Floss gave him an extra point!

In the Trial of Nimbleness, Teggs dodged fifty heat-seeking flying fish thanks to Iggy's super-cool steering. Grandum only dodged *two* before Floss ruled he was clearly the best and gave him *three* extra points!

Worst of all was the Trial of Judgement. Both contestants listened to an argument between two pterodactyls who wanted to fish in the same pond. Teggs thought they should share the spot and take it in turns to go fishing – Joss and Moss gave him two points each. But Grandum said he would blow up the pond so nobody could fish there, to teach them both a lesson. Floss gave him *five* points!

Now they had come to the final test. This was the Trial of Stamina – a hundred-mile flight across the sea and back. Teggs balanced nervously on the starting perch. He was two points behind. But if he won this race the crowd would see he was the overall champion, whatever Floss might say.

"Captain," hissed Iggy through the earpiece. "I don't know if my remote control has enough range for this test. You might go out of control! You might fall and splash into the sea!"

"It's a chance I'll have to take," said Teggs. "We can't give up now!"

Then Gipsy spoke. "Captain! I've just heard from Arx. He knows what's stopping the people from flying. It's a hypno-beam!"

"Of course!" hissed Teggs. "Where is it coming from?"

"He's working that out now. But he thinks Grandum could be behind it."

Teggs glared across at Grandum. "That would explain why *he* can still fly when nobody else can. Not unless they've got robotic wings like me, anyway!"

"Let the Trial begin!" yelled Chief Judge Floss.

Teggs tensed himself for action.

"On your marks – get set – *go*!"

Grandum was away first. Teggs choked on a blast of smelly air from the pterosaur's backside, but soon caught up.

They flew over a range of snow-topped mountains, and out across the sea. It was colder here, and Teggs was glad of his feathers. The grey clouds were blotting out the sun. In fact they hid the whole orange sky from view.

The miles passed by. Slowly, surely, Grandum was pulling ahead.

"Faster, Iggy!" Teggs hissed.

"Sorry, Captain," said Iggy in his ear. "I'm pushing you as fast as I can!"

"Then I'll just have to try surprise tactics," Teggs decided. "Hey, Grandum! The astrosaurs are on to you! They know about your hypno-beam!"

Grandum squawked and spun round in mid-air. "What? No! Impossible!"

"It's true!" Teggs soared past him with a smile. "They will track it down and destroy it. Then everyone will be able to fly again, wherever and whenever they want!"

"They won't!" snarled Grandum. "I won't *let* them — because *I'll* be High Flapper, not you!"

And suddenly, he swooped down and attacked Teggs!

Teggs gasped as Grandum grabbed hold of his feathered tail and shook

him around. He fought back, pecking
Grandum with his false beak.

"Watch those wings, Captain!" hissed
Iggy. "If anything happens to them,
you'll fall!"

Teggs wriggled free of Grandum's
grip. Iggy steered him straight upwards.
"You can hide up here in the clouds,"
he explained. "When Grandum comes
looking, we'll surprise him!"

But it was Teggs who got the
surprise.

He didn't fly
through the clouds.
He bounced *off*
them, head first
– *Klang!*
"Metal clouds?"
thought Teggs
dizzily. The world
whirled around

him. His hidden camera, squashed flat
by the impact, slipped out of his suit.
His brain seemed to rattle in his head
like an acorn in a drum.

"I see you've stumbled upon our little
secret." Grandum laughed nastily. "Or
rather, you've flown straight *into* it!"

Teggs could feel himself passing out.
But before his eyes fell shut he saw a
big, dark hole open up in the clouds
above him . . . and he smelled
Grandum's foul breath as the pterosaur
pushed him inside.

Chapter Eight

THE MAMMOTH MASTERPLAN

Back in the royal carriage, Iggy and
Gipsy were very worried. They'd been
watching their captain's struggles on a
small screen. But now it was blank.

Iggy spoke urgently into the two-way
radio. "Calling
Captain Teggs!
Can you hear me?"
Silence.

"It's no good," he
sighed. "His radio
must be broken.
Either that, or . . ."

"Something terrible happened when
he flew into those clouds!" Gipsy gave

a hoot of alarm. "We have to find him!
But how?"

Sprite looked up from his robotic
wings and chirruped.

Gipsy stared at him. Then she smiled.
"That's a wild idea . . . but it could be
our only chance!"

Teggs woke up in a very strange place.

It looked like a kind of construction
site — but all the builders were woolly
mammoths! There were loads of them,
drilling and digging, sawing and sanding,

leaning on sledgehammers or slurping from great big mugs of tea.

"Gipsy?" he whispered into his radio. "Iggy? Is anyone there?"

But there was no reply.

Another mammoth stomped past close by. He was using his curvy tusks like a screwdriver, putting together some metal rails. In the distance Teggs could see a huge helter-skelter, a ghost train, some swing-boats — and realized that the mammoths beside him were building a rollercoaster! But where in the world was he?

Then he realized he was lying on thick, grey cotton wool. Above him, more clouds were scudding across an expanse of burnt orange.

"I'm up in the sky!" he gasped.

"Who's a clever Flappo, then!" sneered Grandum, looking up from a set of building plans. "That's why we had to stop every pterosaur from flying. So we could build up here in peace!" He scowled. "Our hypno-beam should have worked on everyone. How come you're still flapping about?"

"Perhaps you're not as smart as you think," said Teggs. "Tell me, where *is* this hypno-beam of yours?"

"Nowhere you can get at it," Grandum guffawed. "It's in an empty spaceship, orbiting the planet."

"And the clouds we saw gathering are fakes," Teggs realized. "From down below they look fluffy" He jumped up and down, testing their strength. "But they're really as solid as stone!"

Grandum nodded proudly. "The cloud barrier keeps my building work hidden from prying eyes."

"But just what *are* you building?" Teggs demanded.

"What do you think? A *mammoth* funfair!" Grandum laughed. "Me and the boys, we own the Space-Car Races on Morass Minor. Now we're expanding into theme parks. And since there's no room left on Morass Minor, we're building one on the planet next door instead — right here!"

"But you have no right to build anything on Squawk Major!" said Teggs. "This is not your world!"

"It *will* be, when I become High Flapper!" Grandum grinned. "I'll make sure its people stay flightless forever. The only things in the sky will be my brilliant, noisy, stinky funfair rides, the biggest in the universe. One day, they will stretch right round the planet!"

Teggs glared at him. "I suppose that's the good thing about building in the skies, isn't it? With this cloud barrier to hide you, no one will know what you're up to – until it's too late!"

"Correct." Grandum grinned. "It will also make my funfair *much* easier to keep clean. Every day, a million tourists will turn up, eating and drinking and pooing all over the place. So at night, we'll simply dump all the rubbish over the sides onto the planet below!"

"That's monstrous!" shouted Teggs. "Those poor pterosaurs – like caged canaries, trying to dodge the muck you throw down from above!"

"'Those poor pterosaurs'? You make it sound like you're not one of them." Grandum looked at him suspiciously. "Hey! Your feathers are falling out!"

Teggs gulped. His costume had been torn in the fight with Grandum, and red feathers were littered all around him. A little one caught in his nose and made him sneeze.

"*Aaaaaa-Chooooooo!*"

He sneezed so hard that his false beak fell off!

The mammoths round him gasped. But Grandum only smiled nastily. "So! No wonder the hypno-beam didn't work on you! 'Flappo the Fearless' is only Shazz's pet dinosaur in a suit!"

"My name is Captain Teggs," he replied. "I'm an *astro*saur in a suit! And that means *you* are in big trouble."

Grandum shook his head. "Not when you are in my hidden cloud base, cut off from all your friends!"

Teggs saw twenty ugly mammoths closing in on him. "Ah. You may have a point."

"I brought you here to get you out of the way," said Grandum. "Now no one can stop me becoming High Flapper! I'll tell the judges you got tired and fell in the ocean."

Teggs scoffed. "They'll never believe a story like that!"

"Chief Judge Floss will." Grandum's eyes were gleaming. "Or rather, my mammoth friend who's *pretending* to be Chief Judge Floss will!"

"Of course!" groaned Teggs. "No

wonder Floss suddenly looked and sounded so different. And no wonder he's been giving you points you don't deserve. He's a miserable mammoth in disguise!"

"We had a special Floss costume made, just in case of trouble," said Grandum smugly. "The *real* Chief Judge has been our prisoner since lunch time!"

Teggs glared at him. "You rotten cheats."

"Look who's talking!" cried Grandum. "But don't worry, Teggs. The truth about you will never come out . . . because you will never escape our clutches!"

Teggs tried to run, but the
mammoths were all around him. He
swiped at one with his tail, but his
Flappo disguise was so heavy and
bulky, he couldn't fight very well. Big
feet stomped and kicked him. Long
tusks poked him. Twenty sweaty trunks
held him down.

He knew there was no way out . . .

Chapter Nine

BATTLE IN THE SKY!

Teggs stared furiously at Grandum.
"What are you going to do to me?"

Grandum chuckled. "I'm going to
melt you down in a vat of molten
metal, you dismal dinosaur! You'll end
up as part of a bumper car, or a
candyfloss machine, or a bit of rickety
rollercoaster track . . . "

The mammoths picked Teggs up and
dragged him away, struggling for his
life. The vat of molten metal was close
by, oily and bubbling. Its heat seared
his scaly skin.

"Sorry I can't stay to watch,"
Grandum shouted. "I've got to finish

checking some plans — and then I've
got a race to win."

"My crew will stop you," Teggs told
him. "You'll never succeed!"

"We'll see," said Grandum. "Goodbye,
Teggs! Goodbye forever!"

Teggs heard him flap away.

"We'll throw in the dinosaur on the
count of three, boys," said a very big
mammoth.

"I can't count up to three!" his friend
complained.

The big mammoth sighed. "All right
then, on the count of *two*."

"Is that the one after four?" asked
another.

"No, one is after zero!"

"Shall we throw him in on the count of zero, then?"

"Shut up!" Teggs listened to them squabble. Slowly, he was gathering his strength.

"Look, we won't use numbers, OK?" said the big mammoth. "We'll use letters instead. When we get up to C, we'll throw him in."

A short mammoth scratched his head. "You want us to throw him in the sea?"

"I mean the *letter* C! Now come on. A – B—"

"A bee?" cried the short one. "What bee? Where?"

"A bee! Help, a bee's coming to sting

us!" cried the mammoths.

And while they were panicking, Teggs burst into action.

First, he flapped his robotic wings and scratched the mammoths beside him with his plastic claws.

"We've been stung!" they wailed. "Help!"

Then he flexed his muscles and ripped right through his costume. "Now I've got room to move!" cried Teggs.

He swung his tail with all his strength, and smashed the big mammoth into a half-finished rollercoaster – the whole lot came crashing down. Two more came to get him, trumpeting in fury, but he tripped them up and trod on their trunks.

"There are no bees!" the small mammoth shouted. "Get him!"

Teggs gritted his teeth. The spikes on his back flushed red and he raised his tail. He would show these mammoths what an astrosaur was made of!

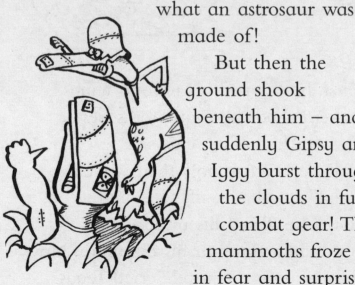

But then the ground shook beneath him – and suddenly Gipsy and Iggy burst through the clouds in full combat gear! The mammoths froze in fear and surprise.

"Guys!" Teggs beamed. "How did *you* get up here?"

"We hitched a lift!", said Gipsy.

And a moment later, fifty daring dimorphodon with robotic wings came flapping inside. Just behind them was the alarm pterosaur in a hang-glider.

Teggs laughed with joy. "Come on, crew! Let's show these mangy mammoths what a team of astrosaurs can do!"

They leaped into action! Iggy's stun-claws sparked and flashed. Gipsy's high-kicks and snout-jabs found their mark. Teggs's tail sliced through the air like a battle-axe. The dimorphodon dive-bombed from above, and the alarm pterosaur squawked at full blast in the mammoths' big hairy ears.

Soon, not one of their foes was left standing.

"Nice work," said Teggs, catching his breath. "But we've got to stop Grandum! You won't believe what he's planning!"

"We will," Iggy assured him. "We heard every word! Your broken radio couldn't *receive* messages, but it still transmitted them!"

"Phew!" sighed Teggs. "Then you know Grandum's hypno-beam is up in orbit?"

Gipsy nodded. "We told Arx. Don't worry, he's on the case!"

Back in the Palace of Perches, Arx looked up from his gadgets with a whoop of joy. "I've found it!" He called the *Sauropod* on his communicator, his horns quivering with excitement.

"This is First Officer Arx. The spaceship carrying the hypno-beam is in sector B-two! Can you locate it?"

"Just looking now," rumbled Alass, the ankylosaurus left in charge. Arx heard her flick some switches. "Aha! Spaceship located!"

"Launch dung torpedoes," cried Arx. "I want it blasted out of the sky!"

"Leave it to me!" said Alass. "Launching torpedoes . . . *now!*"

Arx could hear the distant crump of a huge and very smelly explosion.

"Direct hit!" Alass reported. "We've blasted it right out of the sky, sir, just as you asked. It's on its way down to the planet."

Arx gasped. "But . . . out of the sky

was a figure of speech! I didn't *mean* it!"

"Oh. Sorry sir," said Alass. "But I'm afraid it's going to fall on Squawk Major in just a few minutes!"

"No, it won't," Arx realized. "If it's falling from sector B-two, it'll crash into the mammoths' fake clouds!"

Alass breathed a sigh of relief. "That's all right then!"

"It isn't!" yelled Arx. "Teggs is up there – with Iggy and Gipsy and everyone else!"

Back above the clouds, Teggs and the others were looking for Grandum.

"I hope he hasn't flown off already," said Teggs, as they peeped about from behind a helter-skelter. "Now I've broken my Flappo-suit I can't go after him!"

"No, look!" hooted Gipsy. "There he is!"

Grandum was looking at some funfair blueprints held up by a pair of mammoths.

The alarm pterosaur gave a fierce squawk and launched herself towards him on her hang-glider. She flew right through the blueprints! Grandum gave a cry of alarm.

Teggs smiled grimly. "And those aren't the *only* plans of yours we'll be ruining!"

Grandum gasped. "You!"

"Hope you don't mind, but I've brought a few of my crew along," Teggs said.

Gipsy nodded proudly. "And we're going to bring your high-flying dreams crashing down to earth!"

Never was a truer word spoken.

For at that very moment, the empty spaceship with the hypno-beam on board came whistling down from above like a giant, dung-splattered bullet – heading straight for the middle of the funfair!

"Look out!" Teggs shouted. He and his friends dived for cover behind a big dipper.

The spaceship exploded in a massive ball of flame. The blast wrecked every ride for miles around. The only things still standing were a bit of rollercoaster, half a big wheel and a coconut shy.

Grandum snapped his beak in seething rage. "You have destroyed the hypno-beam – now those pesky pterosaurs will be able to fly again! And just look at my fabulous funfair –

it's ruined!" He fixed the astrosaurs with a terrible stare. "You'll pay for this – with your lives!"

Dozens of mammoth builders, all sooty, singed and scorched, closed in on Teggs and his crew at Grandum's command. But then the ground started to shake. A huge hole opened up in the clouds right by Iggy's feet. He yelped and jumped aside – and almost fell through *another* hole.

Gipsy gasped as a huge split appeared in the clouds beneath her, revealing the snowy mountains below. "What's happening?" she yelled.

"The crashing spaceship has weakened the cloud barrier!" cried Teggs. "That's the only thing holding us up! If it collapses now, this whole place will fall apart!"

"I'm off!" said Grandum.

"Coward!" shouted Teggs. "What about the builders? You can't just leave them behind — you're their boss!"

"Not any more!" he cried. "Mammoths — you're sacked. Happy landings!"

Grandum dived for a gap in the clouds.

"Oh no you don't!" said Teggs, leaping after him.

He landed on the shaggy pterosaur's back. The next thing he knew they were tumbling through the air together.

"Get off me, you fool!" gasped Grandum.

Teggs clung on. "Not a chance!"

"But I can't flap my wings. You'll make us crash!"

"Down we go together!" shouted Teggs, shutting his eyes as they fell faster and faster . . .

Chapter Ten

A FLAPPY ENDING?

Back on Beak Mountain, the echoes of the explosion rumbled like endless thunder. The flock squawked and clattered in alarm. Shazz looked up, her beady eyes full of worry. It sounded like the sky was about to fall in.

And then it did!

The clouds cracked open and started raining down in chunks all around them. The fake Chief Judge Floss hid under a table, wailing like a big baby.

Shazz unfurled her mighty wings and held them up like long, leathery umbrellas. "Listen to me, all of you!" she yelled. "We may not be able to fly, but we can still use our wings – as shields to protect our fellow reptiles! Open them out and keep your heads down! We shall be safe then, you'll see!"

Some little pterosaurs sheltered under her as the strange lumps of cloud kept raining down. Tools and timber, even a coconut or two fell with them. But all the missiles bounced harmlessly off the bigger reptiles' tough, protective wings.

Finally, the bombardment stopped. The thunder ended.

Shazz looked up to see a brilliant orange sky overhead. The sun was shining fat and red, warming the mountain with its light.

A small pterodactyl peeped out from
under one of her wings. "We made it!"
he cheeped. "Three cheers for the High
Flapper, hip-hip—"

"*Squaaaawk!*" bellowed the thankful
flock. They couldn't believe what had
just happened.

But things were about to get even
stranger.

"Look!" someone cried. "It's Grandum
and Flappo! They're coming back!"

"And Flappo's riding on Grandum's
back!"

"That's not Flappo – it's a stegosaurus! Where did *he* come from?"

Shazz gasped. "Oh my goodness!"

Teggs was riding Grandum like a jockey on a horse, clinging on to his neck. The big hairy pterosaur's eyes were bulging as he struggled to keep flapping. "Get off me, you idiot!" he snarled.

"And fall to my doom?" Teggs scoffed. "I really *would* be an idiot then, wouldn't I!"

With a thump, a skid and a rude noise, Grandum landed flat on his beak right in front of the judges' table. He lay in a daze, while Teggs beamed at Joss and Moss. They stared at him in shock.

"Sorry to drop in on you like this!"

he said. "I'm Captain Teggs of the DSS *Sauropod*. And this smelly creature is under arrest!"

Suddenly, Chief Judge Floss burst out from beneath the table. "He is not! He landed back here first — so he's the winner of the Trials! Grandum's the new High Flapper!"

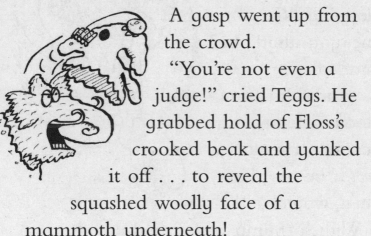

A gasp went up from the crowd.

"You're not even a judge!" cried Teggs. He grabbed hold of Floss's crooked beak and yanked it off . . . to reveal the squashed woolly face of a mammoth underneath!

An even bigger gasp went up from the crowd. A lot of the flock fainted.

Joss cleared his throat. "I'm afraid that even if Chief Judge Floss *is* a mammoth, he's still correct. Grandum has won the trials. And no one can put the High Flapper under arrest. He will rule Squawk Major for ten years!"

Shazz's wings drooped.

But Teggs shook his head. "Rubbish! Grandum can't become High Flapper any more than I can!"

"What do you mean?" Shazz cried.

"I realized when I was riding him here," said Teggs. "I could hear his wings whirring and creaking, and the sound of jet rockets firing. Since when did a true pterosaur need mechanical wings and jet rockets to help him fly?" He grabbed hold of Grandum's ear and pulled hard.

Grandum's face stretched and stretched . . . and pinged off like an old rubber glove.

He was a mammoth too!

The loudest gasp ever recorded rang around Beak Mountain. The pterosaurs that had already fainted woke up and promptly fainted again.

"That's why he smelled so bad," Teggs explained. "A big hairy mammoth squashed into a leather suit for days on end – what a *stink*! And every time he took off he let out filthy fumes from his hidden rockets!"

"But why did he do it?" croaked Shazz.

"Because only a pterosaur can be High Flapper, and he wanted control of your world." He smiled. "I think we should let Grandum explain his entire evil plan later – at his own *trial!*"

Shazz gave a commanding squawk. At once, some burly pterosaurs stepped up to guard the mammoths. "But where is the real Floss?"

"He's here!" panted Arx, lumbering

through the crowd
with the old judge
on his back. Floss
looked startled but
unharmed. "I
found him on my
way here, tied up
and guarded by
a mammoth."

"The beastly
things are
everywhere!" Shazz declared, helping
Floss down.

"Well, I dealt with *that* one, anyway,"
grinned Arx, waggling his horns. "He
should be asleep for some time."

"Well done, Arx." Teggs saluted his
first officer. "You saved the day."

"I'm so glad you saved yourself!"
said Arx. "But what about Gipsy and
Iggy and—"

"Look!" shouted Shazz.

Teggs turned to see an incredible

sight. Three big clouds were sailing through the air towards them, each one towed by a straining flock of dimorphodon using their powerful robotic wings. On one cloud, masses of mammoths huddled together for safety. On another, the alarm pterosaur sat perched atop a big pile of funfair scrap metal. And on the other stood Gipsy and Iggy.

"You made it!" Teggs cheered as the dimorphodon came in to land with their extraordinary load.

"This is all that's left of Grandum's wicked scheme," called Iggy.

"So we thought we should tidy it up," Gipsy added. "Now Squawk Major is left lovely and unpolluted, just like before."

"Not quite," sighed Shazz. "We still can't fly."

"But you *can*!" Arx cleared his throat and called to the crowd. "Grandum was using a hypno-beam to make you think you couldn't fly. That beam has been destroyed, so now your minds should be back to normal!"

A breathless hush settled on the mountain. It was the sound of a million pterosaurs holding their breath, hoping this green triceratops was right.

"Well, go on then," Teggs urged them. "Try it!"

Shazz tried first. She gave her wings a nervous flap and rose up in the air. She flapped them again, and rose higher. And higher . . .

"I'm flying!" she cried. "Look! I'm *flying*!"

"So am I!" cried a pterodactyl, rising from the crowd.

"And me!" squawked Floss. "Look at me! I'm shaking my booty!"

Teggs laughed. Soon the air was filled

with flying reptiles, squawking and
screeching with joy. The dimorphodon
pecked off their mechanical wings and
the alarm pterosaur chucked away her
hang-glider. They looped the loop
round Gipsy and Iggy, and buzzed past
Teggs and Arx in a blissful blur.

None of the astrosaurs had seen a
sight so wonderful in all their lives.

"Well, Arx," said Teggs. "This planet's
problems are solved. Its people can live
flappily ever after!"

Arx nodded. "And once a new High Flapper is chosen, Shazz can enjoy a nice long holiday." He paused. "Come to think of it, *we* could use a holiday too!"

"Holiday?" Teggs pulled a face. "Forget it! There's just time for a quick celebration dinner, then it's back to the *Sauropod*." He smiled. "Even over all that squawking, I can hear the call of another adventure! Can't you?"

THE END

TALKING DINOSAUR!

How to say the dinosaur and pterosaur names in this book . . .

ANKYLOSAUR –
an-KI-*loh*-SORE

STYGIMOLOCH –
STIJ-*i*-MOH-*lok*

PTEROSAUR –
TEH-*roh-sore*

DIMORPHODON –
die-MORF-*oh-don*

TRICERATOPS –
try-SERRA-*tops*

NYCTOSAURUS –
NIK-*toh*-SORE-*rus*

QUETZALCOATLUS –
kwet-zal-COAT-*lus*

RHAMPHORHYNCHUS –
RAM-*foh*-RING-*kus*

SORDES –
SORE-*deez*

PTERODACTYL –
teh-roh-DACT-*il*

ASTROSAURS

BOOK SIX

THE SPACE GHOSTS

Read the first chapter here!

Chapter One
THE CURSED TREASURE

The shuttle swooped out of the night sky, like a metal egg falling from a nest of stars. It zoomed over the surface of a barren planet. There was no sign of life. Nothing but rocks and stones, slowly crumbling to dust.

The shuttle landed and Teggs Stegosaur stuck out his inquisitive beak.

"So this is the planet Creepus,'" he said. It was cold and creepy. The wind howled. Stone and shingle scrunched beneath his four feet. Anything could be hiding in the caves and canyons of this lonely world.

Teggs smiled to himself. It was just

the sort of place for an adventure!

Arx followed him out of the shuttle. "Not a nice place for a picnic," he noted, ducking his large frilly head as the wind blew sand in his eyes. "Luckily, Camp Kentro is not far from here."

"I've got the tracker," called Gipsy Saurine. As she stepped out to join her crewmates, the tracker on her wrist was already bleeping. "This will lead us straight to Camp Kentro."

"Where Shanta and his diplodocus crew will be waiting to give us a nice cup of swamp tea," said Arx. "I hope!"

They set off through the stinging wind, and Teggs thought about their mission. Shanta Digg was a famous diplodocus miner. He and his team had worked in mines all across the Jurassic Quadrant. They had dug for diamonds on Diplos. And they had come here to Creepus in search of something very special indeed ...

But they had found only problems. Shanta had called the DSS for help, and Admiral Rosso, the head of the DSS, had sent the Sauropod straight here. What help did the miners need?

After trudging through the wilderness for several minutes, Teggs saw some battered buildings in the valley below. They looked old and deserted in the silvery moonlight – and very spooky.

Gipsy checked her tracker. "That must be Camp Kentro."

"Come on!" Teggs charged off towards the bundle of old buildings. "Let's go!"

A few minutes later they reached the camp. Iggy jabbed his thumb spike on the doorbell.

"Who's there?" a voice whispered.

"Captain Teggs and his fellow astrosaurs!" said Teggs.

A minute later the door slid open. A

sleek head the size of a rugby ball pushed out at them.

Teggs recognized the diplodocus at once. "Shanta Digg?"

"Aye, my lad," said Shanta, looking about nervously. "That's me. Now, come inside, quick. And close the door behind you!"

Arx frowned. "He seems a bit jittery."

"Yes, what's up, Shanta?" said Iggy, walking inside. "You look like you've seen a ghost."

"Ghost?" cried Shanta. He banged his head on the ceiling in surprise and started to stammer. "W-w-what ghost? Where?"

"Nowhere!" said Gipsy. "It was just a figure of speech."

"F-f-figure? What figure?" The whole camp shook as he stamped round and round in a tizzy. "Plod, quick! There's another figure!"

"Not another one!" Plod, a slightly larger diplodocus, swung her neck round the corner. "Where is it? What was it doing? Who—"

"There's no one here but us!" yelled Teggs. His sudden outburst stopped the diplodocus in their tracks. "Now, what is going on around here?"

Read the rest of
THE SPACE GHOSTS
to find out what spooky
adventures face the astrosaurs!

Find your fantastic **ASTROSAURS** collector cards in the back of this book. Four more cards are available in each **ASTROSAURS** book. You can also add to your collection by looking at

www.astrosaurs.co.uk